Some Bunny To Talk To

A Story About Going to Therapy

by Cheryl Sterling, PhD, Paola Conte, PhD,
and Larissa Labay, PsyD

illustrated by Tiphanie Beeke

MAGINATION PRESS • WASHINGTON, DC
American Psychological Association

Published by
MAGINATION PRESS
An Educational Publishing Foundation Book
American Psychological Association
750 First Street, NE
Washington, DC 20002

For more information about our books, including a
complete catalog, please write to us, call 1-800-374-2721,
or visit our website at www.apa.org/pubs/magination.

Book design by Susan K. White
Printed by Phoenix Color Corporation, Hagerstown, MD

Library of Congress Cataloging-in-Publication Data
Sterling, Cheryl, 1968– author.
Some Bunny to talk to : a story about going to therapy /
by Cheryl Sterling, PhD, Paola Conte, PhD,
and Larissa Labay, PsyD ; illustrated by Tiphanie Beeke.
pages cm
"American Psychological Association."
Summary: When Little Bunny's problem makes him feel sad and
fearful, he goes to a therapist for help. Includes note to parents.
ISBN 978-1-4338-1649-9 (hardcover) — ISBN 1-4338-1649-0
(hardcover) — ISBN 978-1-4338-1650-5 (pbk.) —
ISBN 1-4338-1650-4 (pbk.) [1. Psychotherapy—Fiction.
2. Rabbits—Fiction.] I. Conte, Paola, author. II. Labay, Larissa,
author. III. Beeke, Tiphanie, illustrator. IV. Title.
PZ7.S8373So 2015
[E]—dc23 2013048000

Manufactured in the United States of America

10 9 8 7 6 5 4 3 2 1

Little Bunny had a problem. A big one.
And he didn't know how to solve it.
It seemed too big for a little bunny like him.

It seemed too big for his bunny friends, and even too big for Big Bunny. He was worried and sad. Kind of like that time before he knew how to ride a bike. He didn't even know how to start trying and he didn't think he could ever learn.

Sometimes things in a little bunny's life can feel so hard.

The
N
W
E
S

Little Bunny was starting to be nervous and scared about lots of things. He was afraid of thunderstorms and nighttime. And being alone. At bedtime, Little Bunny worried and this made it hard for him to sleep.

Big Bunny tried to help. “Count carrots,” she said.

“Tried! That doesn’t work,” said Little Bunny.

“Think of good things,” she said.

“That won't work either,” said Little Bunny.

No ideas
were working!
This made
Little Bunny
disappointed.

"Why can't I feel like I used to when I just thought about hopping and fun? I'll never feel like that again!" Little Bunny started to cry.

Big Bunny had an idea. Big Bunny wanted to help Little Bunny, but she knew she needed help from some bunny else.

“I have an idea. I'd like you to talk to Some Bunny. Some Bunny is a therapist.”

"A therapist is a person whose job it is
to help bunnies like you solve problems.
They don't have all the answers,
but they are really good at helping
you figure out what a good answer
may be for you."

Little Bunny said, "You mean a therapist
can help me figure out what's been
bugging me? And help me feel better?

But why can't I just talk to:

"Sometimes a bunny who doesn't
see you all the time can help you think
of new ideas to solve a problem.
Then you can practice ways to make
hard times easier and get back to being
my little bunny!" said Big Bunny.

"Here are some other things to know:

Therapists ask
lots of questions,
but like to listen
to you even more.

Therapists
help you
feel safe and
comfortable.

Therapists love to
play games or draw."

"Your therapist will ask you some questions about the things you like to do so you can get to know each other better," said Big Bunny. "You can ask your therapist questions, too. Maybe you will find out that you have the same favorite color."

Little Bunny started to think.

Really?
I like purple
too!

Carrots are
my favorite,
but I also love
cupcakes!

Big Bunny said, "Do you know how it feels when you are giving your teddy bear a giant hug? You feel happy and relaxed. Your therapist will help you think of ways to feel comfortable and safe, even when you're not hugging your teddy bear."

Little Bunny thought some more.

Ahh,
feels good.
1. . . 2. . . 3. . .
smile.

Big Bunny said, "You might play a game or draw a picture. Then Some Bunny can help you think of ideas to help you feel better."

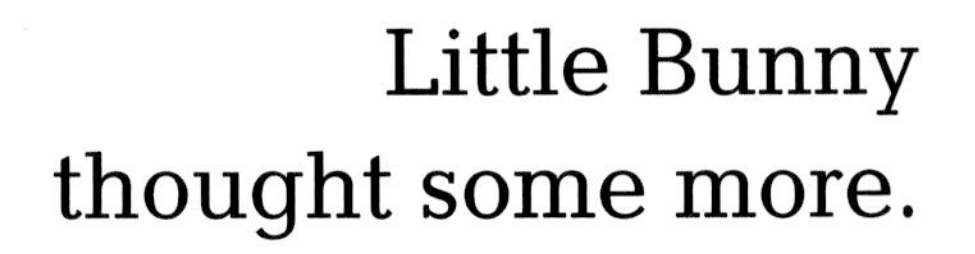

Little Bunny thought some more.

That looks just like I imagined.

Big Bunny said, "Do you know what **PRIVATE** means? Private has to do with something you keep all to yourself. You, your therapist, and I are the only ones who know what you talk about. And even though you can tell other bunnies if you and I decide it is OK, your therapist won't tell anyone about your conversations or that you come in to talk."

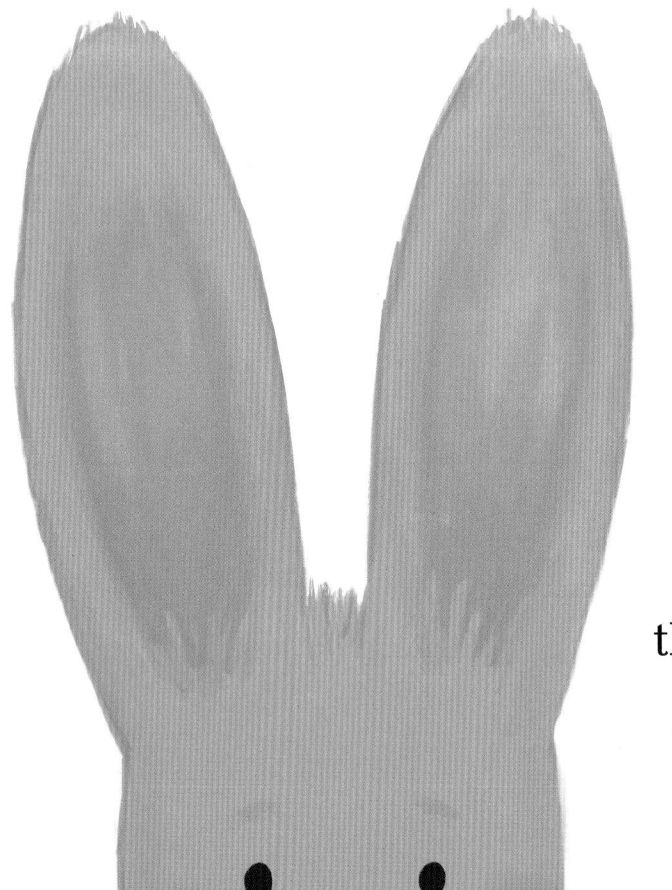

Little Bunny thought some more.

Dr. Bunny
Therapist
Private

Little Bunny asked,
"How many times will I go?"

Big Bunny explained, "Probably
your therapist, you, and I will decide.
You will probably go more than once,
but less than a gazillion times.
You will go for as long as it takes
for you to feel like yourself again.
Maybe we can try to make
a guess with your therapist and
see who is the closest."

Little Bunny
thought some more.

1. . . 2. . . 3. . .
I'm thinking of a number between 1 and a gazillion.

"How long will I be there?" asked Little Bunny

"Each week you will start at a certain time and end at a certain time. Usually you will be there for about 45 minutes. Another way to say this is ¾ of an hour."

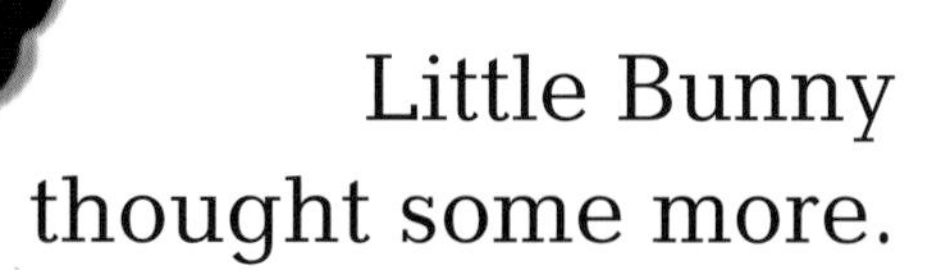

Little Bunny thought some more.

That's nothing! I can eat 5 peanut butter and jelly sandwiches in 45 minutes.
nutty
Wonder how many pictures I can draw?

Both Little Bunny and Big Bunny were
feeling a little better because they talked.

"It's great to talk and really great
to know that talking to a therapist can help a little
bunny solve problems," said Big Bunny.

Little Bunny said, "Yes, talking to
Some Bunny will really help!"

Note to Parents & Caregivers

From time to time families face difficult life circumstances, and as adults we may recognize the need to seek help from a professional therapist. When our children face similar challenges, parents may also choose to enlist the services of an experienced child therapist. Seeing a therapist can often be the best strategy to help your child through a difficult time. While families reach this decision in different ways at different times, parents can think of psychotherapy services for their child as they would any other helpful resource. Choosing to bring your child to a therapist is a proactive and productive choice.

HOW THIS BOOK CAN HELP

Whether you are considering or have already decided to bring your child to a therapist, *Some Bunny To Talk To* presents therapy in a way that is simple, direct, and easy for young children to understand. This colorful, humorous book is designed to help you answer your children's questions and allay everyone's fears about the process of therapy. Children will hear about what to expect from therapy and how therapists can help people solve problems. They will learn about confidentiality and privacy and understand the process of therapy from the first visit to how the decision may be made to end therapy.

HOW TO PAVE THE WAY FOR A POSITIVE THERAPY EXPERIENCE

Once you have decided to seek therapy for your child, you may want to ask a trusted professional for a recommendation. Your pediatrician, your child's teacher, or a school counselor can be excellent resources for suggestions about skilled therapists in your area.

Choose a good match. Therapeutic success is highly influenced by the match between the therapist and your child. Not every therapist is right for every child. Meet with the therapist prior to your child's first meeting to gauge your comfort with the therapist's style and approach to therapy. You should ask the therapist about his or her experience working with children as well as with your child's particular issue. It is often helpful to ask how the therapist will approach this issue with your child. Try to gauge how the therapist typically assesses the problem, formulates a treatment plan, and implements treatment, as well as how much they incorporate parents or caregivers in the treatment process. Remember, it is important that you feel comfortable with the extent to which you will be involved in the treatment, and your input is valuable throughout the duration of therapy. It is okay to ask any question you feel would be important in the decision making process. It is preferable for all primary caregivers to attend the initial meeting and to be actively involved in the choice of therapist. It is always an option to choose a different therapist at any time. However, we recommend that the decision to change therapists not be made impulsively. It is worth having a conversation with the therapist about any reservations or concerns that may develop.

Prepare your child for therapy. Once you have chosen a therapist, prepare your child for his first meeting. Begin by telling him that he will be meeting a feelings doctor (or feelings person). This is someone who does not wear a white coat or give any needles, but who is very good at helping to make sad or scary feelings less uncomfortable. Therapists are skilled at helping people to solve problems. For children who may be afraid of going to the pediatrician, you could explain that a therapist is like a teacher or coach whose job it is to teach kids ways to make the harder things in their lives easier. Keep your preparations brief. Parents may introduce the idea of therapy first and then read the book, or they can read the book as a way of introducing a decision that has already been made about seeing a therapist. It may also be useful to read this book once treatment has been initiated to clarify any questions that may occur regarding the process of therapy.

Engage your child. While going to therapy is a decision best made thoughtfully and seriously, introducing the idea to children may seem difficult at first. However, children are usually much more amenable and interested in therapy if it can be seen as helpful, entertaining, and useful. Parents frequently feel anxious about the process of therapy themselves and may present some of their own anxiety to children unknowingly. Many usual barriers to engaging children and adolescents in therapy are those same barriers experienced by adults: the idea that therapy is for "bad" or troubled people, the stigma about "being crazy," and the idea that therapists are boring, scary, or weird. Kids might not understand why they need to go. If questions along these lines come up, reassure your child that therapy is positive and that sometimes kids need a little bit of help getting through rough patches. You might even tell your child that therapists talk with researchers and other experts to figure out the best ways to make the harder things in life feel easier for lots of people.

Show confidence and enthusiasm. After meeting with the therapist, you will bring your child in for an initial session. It is not uncommon to see resistance from your child regarding this visit. Remember that you should treat any hesitation on your child's part in the same way you might respond to a child who complains about going to school. You should be supportive yet firm because your child will take your lead. If you show confidence and enthusiasm while communicating your expectation that the visit will go well, your child will be more comfortable and you will likely see ongoing cooperation.

Support your child in therapy. All primary caregivers should be actively included in their child's therapy. Parents typically serve as coaches between therapy sessions. You should also be receiving regular feedback about your child's treatment and progress. Do not hesitate to ask for this if you feel you would like to receive information more frequently. While this book is geared towards individual treatment for children, there may be times when a whole family would benefit from participating in family therapy.

We hope you find that *Some Bunny To Talk To* paves the way for a positive, stress-free first therapy experience for you and your child.

About the Authors

Cheryl Sterling, PhD, Paola Conte, PhD, and **Larissa Labay, PsyD,** are pediatric psychologists in private practice who specialize in providing cognitive-behavioral therapy to children and adolescents. They trained at Brown and Harvard University, the University of Miami, and the Children's Hospital of Philadelphia, respectively. Cheryl Sterling and Larissa Labay are on staff at a major medical center in Northern New Jersey, while Paola Conte practices on Long Island, NY.

About the Illustrator

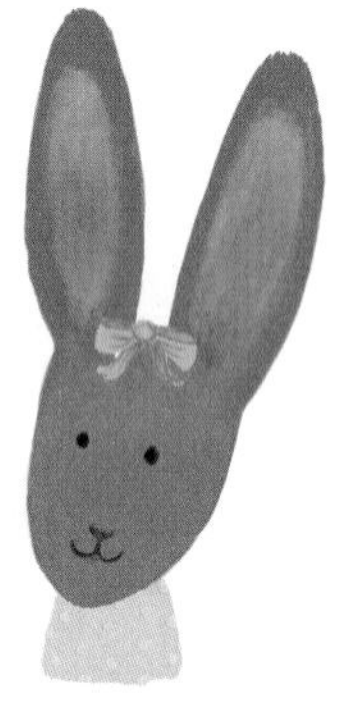

Tiphanie Beeke earned a master's degree in illustration from the Royal College of Art in London and currently lives in France with her husband and three children. She enjoys the sunshine, the snow, illustrating books, and living with her noisy family.

About Magination Press

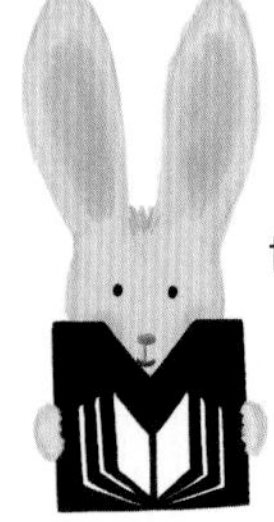

Magination Press publishes self-help books for kids and the adults in their lives. Magination Press is an imprint of the American Psychological Association, the largest scientific and professional organization representing psychologists in the United States and the largest association of psychologists worldwide.